Books about Judy Moody and Stink
by Megan McDonald, illustrated by Peter H. Reynolds

Judy Moody & Stink

The Big Bad BlacKout

Megan McDonald
illustrated by Peter H. Reynolds

Text copyright © 2014 by Megan McDonald
Illustrations copyright © 2014 by Peter H. Reynolds
Judy Moody font copyright © 2003 by Peter H. Reynolds

Judy Moody®. Judy Moody is a registered trademark
of Candlewick Press, Inc.
Stink®. Stink is a registered trademark of Candlewick Press, Inc.

First edition 2014

Library of Congress Catalog Card Number
2013943995
ISBN 978-0-7636-6520-3

14 15 16 17 18 19 TLF 10 9 8 7 6 5 4 3 2 1
Printed in Dongguan, Guangdong, China

This book was typeset in Stone
Informal and Judy Moody.
The illustrations were created
digitally.

Candlewick Press
99 Dover Street
Somerville, Massachusetts 02144

visit us at www.candlewick.com

For Lovey

M. M.

To Eloise and Jack Cheever

P. H. R.

CONTENTS

Bump! Thwump!

"Ghost!" Judy yelped, bolting awake from a crash on the roof. Her heart beat louder than a ticking clock. "That sounded like a giant bionic squirrel landing on the roof, Mouse. Or all nine of Santa's reindeer."

Mouse covered an ear with one paw.

Ba-bump-bump-bump.

"Eeeeee! What if it *is* a ghost? And he's bowling—up in the attic!" Judy held her cat close. "Don't be scared, Mouse. I'll protect you."

Judy scrambled down from her top bunk and grabbed a Grouchy pencil and her Women of Science ruler. Brandishing one in each hand, she rushed out the door and bumped headlong into . . .

Stink! He waved a lightsaber and yelled, "The sky is falling! The sky is falling!"

"Hey, Chicken Little! Did you hear what I just heard?" Judy asked.

"If you mean the giant spaceship that just crash-landed on the roof, I heard it." Judy and Stink flew down the stairs, Mouse at their heels. They skidded into the kitchen on sock feet, looking for Mom and Dad.

Computer? On. TV? On. But no Mom or Dad.

Just then, Mom came out of the laundry room, tugging on her rubber boots.

"Ghost!" Judy pointed to the attic with her ruler.

"Spaceship!" said an out-of-breath Stink.

"Bionic squirrel! Reindeer!" Judy spouted.

"Alien! Invasion!" Stink hiccupped.

"Crash landing!" Judy sputtered.

"Roof!" Stink nodded.

"It's this storm," said Mom. "The wind has kicked up like crazy. Dad's outside checking the roof right now." Mom shrugged on her raincoat and grabbed an umbrella. "You kids sit tight. I'm going out to look, too." She opened the back door to step out, and a flurry of wet leaves blew in.

"Great," said Stink. "Aliens just crash-landed right here in Frog Neck Lake, Virginia, and we're supposed to sit tight."

⟖   ⟖   ⟖

Rain, rain, and more rain. Rain drummed on the roof. Rain hammered against the house. Judy watched it run in rivers down the windows.

When she turned around, Stink had his ear pressed up to a . . . flashlight? A talking flashlight!

"AlleyOop Charter, Clara Barton Elementary, Crabtree Elementary, closed."

"What did the flashlight say to the second grader?" Judy teased.

Stink looked up. "I don't know? What?"

"It's not a joke, Stink. You're listening to . . . a flashlight?"

"Hardee-har-har. It's a flashlight, but it's also a radio." He jiggled the antenna. "I'm trying to find out if school's canceled."

Wind rattled the back door. "It's not a snow day, Stink. Whoever heard of a *rain* day?"

"It could happen," said Stink.

"Yeah, right. And pencils grow on trees."

"Uh . . . pencils *are* made from trees," said Stink.

"Oh. Right."

"*Franklin Elementary, Hall Elementary, closed.*" Stink crossed his fingers on both hands.

"Say *Virginia Dare Elementary!*" he shouted at the radio.

"It's raining cats and dogs out there," said Mom, coming through the back door, her umbrella turned inside out.

"Any guinea pigs?" Stink asked slyly.

"Dad's still trying to find out what made that awful noise on the roof. I couldn't see a thing."

"*Our Lady of Peace School, Plum Creek Middle School — closed.*"

Dad came in the back door next, dripping a pond-sized puddle on the floor.

"So?" asked Stink. "Was it a spaceship?"

"Or Santa?" said Judy.

"Aliens?"

"Reindeer?"

"Guinea pigs?"

"Tent," said Dad, shaking water from his hair like a dog. "Your Toad Pee Club tent was up on the roof."

"You mean to say the wind picked up the tent and blew it all the way across the yard," Stink said, waving his arms wildly, "and then—*bing, bang, boom!*—up on the roof?"

"Yep," said Dad.

"Whoa. Crash landing! Just like the house in *The Wizard of Oz*," said Judy.

"Now we'll have to have our club meetings up on the roof!" Stink said with a grin.

"No, I got the tent down," said Dad. "But this is no ordinary storm. Weather report said winds are over forty miles per hour and we've had several inches of rain already. Looks like we might be in for a hurricane."

Judy's eyes grew wide.

Stink looked from Dad to Mom.

Dad turned up the TV. "It's official. What we hoped was just a tropical storm has just been upgraded to hurricane status," the weatherman reported. "Batten down the hatches, folks. Hurricane Elmer is heading straight for the East Coast."

"Hurricane!" cried Stink. "Shouldn't we be doing something? Boiling water?"

"That's if a baby's coming, Stink. Isn't it, Mom?"

"Then we should be breathing into a paper bag or something."

"That's for hiccups," said Judy.

"Stand in a doorway?"

"Earthquakes, Stink."

"*Silver Lake Middle School, Skipwith Academy, Wee Ones Preschool, closed. This just in: Frog Neck Lake . . .*"

"Shh!" Stink put the flashlight up to his ear.

"... *Public Library, Frog Neck Lake Senior Center* ..."

"Aw," said Stink. "They're never going to say our school."

"Kids? You'd better get ready," said Mom. "If there is school, you're already going to be late."

"*Frog Neck Lake School District* ... *including Virginia Dare Elementary School—closed.*"

Stink looked at Judy. Judy looked at Stink.

"No school?" Stink asked.

"No school!" said Judy.

"Woo-hoo!" Judy and Stink high-fived, low-fived, middle-fived, and then they danced around the kitchen.

Later that morning, Mrs. Moody made a quick trip to the grocery store. When she came back, Stink stood on tiptoe, peering into the bags. "Did you get marshmallows?"

"I got marshmallows," said Mom. "They were out of tuna fish and soup and cereal, but they still had marshmallows. The shelves were almost bare with everybody stocking up for the storm."

"I guess we'll have to eat marshmallow soup," said Judy.

"Mmm. I don't care," said Stink. "I

could *live* in a house of marshmallows."

Dad carried a giant blue water bottle in from the car. "Who lives in a house of marshmallows?" he asked.

"Grandma Lou!" Stink yelled.

"What? Grandma Lou doesn't—" Judy started.

"No, I forgot," said Stink. "I was supposed to tell you guys that Grandma Lou called. She's on her way here to stay with us."

"Good. Because Virginia Beach is getting slammed," said Dad.

"Stink said her power already went out," Judy reported.

"She had to leave or they were going to evaporate her!" said Stink.

"I think it's *evacuate*," said Mom. "I'm glad she left when she did. If they closed the bridge in high winds, she'd be stuck."

"Poor Grandma Lou always seems to be in the teeth of the storm," said Dad.

"And," said Stink, "I'm supposed to tell you she's not alone."

Mom raised an eyebrow at Dad. "Oh?"

"Who's she bringing?" Dad asked.

"Somebody named . . . Gert. And Pugsy and some other names, too. I can't remember."

"Maybe Grandma Lou has an evil twin named Gert and they were separated at birth and she's bringing her here and Evil Gert will cast an evil spell on us," Judy said all in one breath.

Dad laughed. "I hate to break this to you, but Gert is short for *Gertrude.* And *Gertrude* is Grandma Lou's kayak."

"Grandma Lou has a boat named *Gert?*" said Judy.

"See, right before Grandpa Jack died, he told Grandma Lou, 'Whatever you do, don't be an old Gertrude.' So Grandma Lou went out and got herself a kayak. To help her stay young. She named it *Gert.* Short for *Gertrude.*"

"Phew," said Stink. "A boat's way better than an evil twin."

Dad turned up the TV. "Sounds like they think Elmer will hit land later tonight on the Outer Banks of North Carolina," Dad said.

Outside, the wind howled. Mouse leaped from her perch on top of the fridge to the floor and made a dash for the laundry room.

"The storm is freaking her out," said Stink.

"Storms and vacuum cleaners," said Judy. "Those make her run and hide in the laundry basket, under all the clothes."

"Not the clean clothes, I hope," said Mom. "Kids? You'll have to bunk together with Grandma Lou coming. Judy, you can sleep in Stink's room for a few nights."

Stink pumped his fist in the air. "Yes, yes, yes!"

"No, no, nooooo," Judy groaned.

"No moaning," said Mom.

"Fine. There's already a ghost in my room anyway."

"You have a lot to do to get your room picked up before Grandma Lou gets here," Mom pointed out.

"Ha, ha." Stink was pointing at Judy. "School's out and you have to clean your room!"

"Stink, you need to pick up your room, too," said Mom.

"Ha, ha to you," said Judy.

"I can't pick up my room," said Stink.

"Why not?" Mom asked.

"It's too heavy!" said Stink. He cracked himself up again.

*B*eep-beep-beep! *Hooonk!* Stink and Judy ran to the front window. The rain made a Morse code of dots and dashes on the panes. Wind bent the trees sideways. A yellow Mini had pulled into the driveway. A red kayak was strapped to the roof.

"Grandma Lou's here!" called Judy and Stink.

Holding a newspaper over her head, Grandma Lou made a mad dash for the front door, puddle-jumping and splashing all the way.

"Kiddos!" Grandma Lou squeezed them in a big hug. "Am I glad to see you!"

"Hey! You're getting us all wet," said Stink.

"How was your trip, Mom?" Dad asked.

"Crazy!" said Grandma Lou. "The waves are yay high and there's flooding in the streets. Everybody's heading inland, so the bridge was bumper-to-bumper traffic all the way."

"We're glad you're here safe and sound," said Mom. "C'mon in and dry off."

"First things first," said Grandma Lou, and reached into her tote bag. Then she pulled out a wet pug and set him on the floor.

"Pugsy!" cried Judy and Stink. Pugsy shook himself off.

"Kids, keep an eye on Pugs for a minute. Be back in a flash." Grandma Lou dashed through the rain to her car again.

Pugsy jumped and bounced and ran through the kids' legs, playing tag.

"Wonder who else she brought," Mom said, moving aside the curtain to see.

Grandma Lou came back with a Critter Keeper in each hand. "This is Milo," she said, holding up one of the crates. Two black eyes, a pink nose, and a black-and-white striped face peered out.

"P.U.! Skunk!" yelled Stink, pinching his nose shut.

"He's not a skunk. He's a ferret," said Grandma Lou. "And this," she said holding up the other carryall, "is Candy Cane."

"Snake!" yelled Stink. Everybody backed up.

"Don't worry, she's friendly," said Grandma Lou. "She's a corn snake."

"A corn snake named Candy Corn?" Stink asked. "Weird."

"Candy *Cane*," said Judy. "I get it. Because she has red-and-white stripes."

"Somebody sure got pranked when they looked in their Christmas stocking," said Stink. "Hey, wait. The

snake's sleeping in your room, right, Grandma Lou?"

"Sure. The snake will make a good foot warmer!" Grandma Lou teased.

"So, you brought a zoo," said Dad. "Anything else we should know?"

"I know. I'm sorry," said Grandma Lou. "I'm pet sitting. My neighbors are waiting out the storm at a shelter that won't take pets, so they asked me to help. I could hardly say no."

"You got skunked!" said Stink.

"You won't even know they're here. I promise."

"A snake in the house? I'll know," Mom teased. "Judy, take Grandma Lou up to your room."

"You carry Milo's crate," said Grandma Lou. "I'll carry the snake." She followed Judy upstairs.

"This is my bunk bed," said Judy. "You can sleep on top or bottom. I'll be rooming with Stink." She made a sour-ball face.

"Sorry about that. You're welcome to bunk with me."

"That's okay."

Judy pointed to her bookshelves. "These are my books. You can read them, but if there's a bookmark, don't lose my place."

"I hate when that happens," said Grandma Lou.

"I'll clear my desk off for Candy Cane," said Judy. "But don't let her get too close to my Venus flytrap. Jaws likes to snap!"

"I'll remember that," said Grandma Lou.

"This is my Band-Aid collection. You can use some, but ask me first. And here's my pizza-table collection — don't let Pugsy chew them, like last time."

Grandma Lou nodded. "I'm sure Pugsy and I will be very comfy."

"*And* Milo *and* Candy Cane," said Judy. "It sure is zooey in here!"

🌀　🌀　🌀

That afternoon, while Grandma Lou took a nap, Judy and Stink played fetch with Pugsy and Mouse. Judy and Stink took Milo for a walk — around the downstairs. "How do you play with a snake?" Stink asked.

"You don't," said Judy.

Rain slashed the windows and thrum-drummed on the roof. "The storm is headed straight for Ocracoke," said the TV. "It could hit land in the next few hours."

When Grandma Lou woke up, she helped Judy and Stink write a message in a bottle. It said *Come over after the storm* in secret code.

Judy ran outside and set it free in the storm drain. "It should reach Rocky by tomorrow," she told them.

All of a sudden, the lights blinked. Off. On. Off. On.

Thunder rumbled low like a car engine, and lightning cracked the sky. The lights flickered. The lights dimmed. The lights came back on.

Stink looked at the ceiling. "Grandma Lou? If you're sleeping tonight and you happen to hear a loud crash on the roof, don't be scared. It's probably not aliens."

"Or reindeer," said Judy. "Or a giant bionic squirrel."

"And it's probably not Bigfoot," said Stink. "Just so you know."

"Or Sasquatch. Or the Skunk Ape," said Judy.

"Good to know," said Grandma Lou.

"It's probably just a regular old ghost," Judy teased.

Whoooo! All of a sudden, the lights went out again. The room turned ink black. The TV fell silent. It felt like the house was under a magic spell. Outside, the wind whooshed like waves pounding the shore. Chimes clanged and rain poured.

The scary dark sent chills up Judy's spine.

"Ooh, blackout!" cried Stink. "A big bad blackout!"

I'll get the candles," said Mom.

"I'll get the flashlights," said Dad.

"I'll get the marshmallows!" said Stink.

Outside, the storm flashed and crashed. Pugsy yipped and yapped. Milo ran in circles around the room.

Judy and Grandma Lou felt their way to the front window and peered outside. "The whole street is black," said Judy.

"Looks like the storm knocked out power to the whole neighborhood," said Grandma Lou.

"Spooky!" said Stink. "No electricity—no lights, no computer, no TV. That means—*waah!*—I can't play the *Mad Muskrats* physics-based castle demolition game."

"No computer mini golf or bowling games either," said Judy.

"But also no bath," Stink chirped, "and no homework!"

Mom brought candles set in tuna-fish cans to the table.

"We're pioneers," said Stink. "Like Abe Lincoln in his log cabin! Except instead of coyotes and mountain lions, there are ferrets and candy-cane snakes."

Mom went to look for more candles. Dad started a fire in the fireplace. The

house seemed extra snug in the dark. Outside, the wind howled.

"I'm bored," said Stink.

"You're not bored," said Judy. "You're never bored."

"I know. But it's dark and nobody's said anything for a while."

"There are lots of things we can do by candlelight," said Grandma Lou. "I could teach you to knit. We could make knitted zombies!"

A tree limb cracked outside the window. Stink shivered. "No, thanks," he said.

"We could play cards. How about Cuckoo Canasta?"

"But we only have three people," said Judy.

"I know," said Grandma Lou. "Let's play a board game."

"Cluedo!" said Judy.

"Too scary," said Stink. "Scrabble?"

"Too long," said Judy. "How about Chinese checkers?"

"You always win," said Stink. "Maybe Trouble?"

"*You* always win," said Judy. "Let's play Sorry!"

"Wow," said Grandma Lou. "I'm *sorry* I caused so much *trouble.* We could be here all night trying to make up our minds."

"Abe Lincoln played marbles," said Stink.

"Tell you what. Let's play Musical Board Games," Grandma Lou said.

"Wha? Huh?" said Judy and Stink.

"Musical Board Games. It's Abe Lincoln approved. You know Musical Chairs? You each get to pick two board games. We'll set up all four games around the room."

"Four games!" said Judy.

"I'll turn on the music and you start playing one game. When I stop the music, you move to the next game. It goes really fast."

"That's cuckoo-berry!" said Stink.

"Cuckoo-berry times four!" said Judy.

"Let's play," said Stink, bouncing up and down. "No. Wait. Can't. There's no power. How are we going to play music?"

Grandma Lou dug in her bag. "One thing you should know about your old

grandma. She never leaves home without . . ."

"A deck of cards?" asked Stink.

"Cough drops?" asked Judy.

"Batteries!"

"Stink, go get Dad's old CD player,"
Judy said.

Judy and Stink played Musical Board
Games till they were out of breath. Pugsy
chased after Judy and Stink, and Milo
chased after Pugsy. Mouse watched the
whole thing. Then they played Spit in the
Ocean and Old Maid (which Grandma
Lou made them call Not-So-Old Granny).

"Let's read a book," said Grandma Lou.

"It's too dark," said Judy and Stink at
the same time.

"Jinx! One - two - three - four - five - six - seven!" said Judy. "You owe me a hot chocolate, Stink!"

"Too bad the stove doesn't work in the blackout. Ha, ha!"

Grandma Lou rummaged through her bag and pulled out a book. *"Candlelight Stories!* This was your dad's book when he was your age."

"Coolsville," said Stink. "Abe Lincoln didn't have electricity in his log cabin, so he read books by candlelight, too."

Grandma Lou read a fairy tale about a mouse, a bird, and a talking sausage! While she read, Stink folded origami boats. Mouse toyed with them. When Judy made a hurricane flip book out of sticky notes, Pugsy tried to chew it.

"Weird!" said Stink. "I bet Abe Lincoln did not have a book about a talking sausage. I never knew it could be so fun without a computer."

"Or lights," said Judy.

"Or a TV or video games," said Stink.

Stink got out his markers and made a poster about nine things to do in a blackout.

Dad tried Stink's flashlight radio, but he couldn't get a signal. "I'll try the radio in the car." When he came back, he said, "Sounds like they closed half the streets in town. We may need *Gert* just to get you two to school tomorrow."

"School?" said Judy.

"*School?*" said Stink.

"Just kidding!" said Dad. "Actually, they may need the school for a shelter, so it'll probably be a few days."

"Yippee!" yelled Stink and Judy.

◎　◎　◎

When it was time for dinner, Dad asked, "What should we have? Peanut-butter-and-marshmallow sandwiches?"

"I did manage to get bread, eggs, and baked beans at the store," said Mom.

"Silver-dollar pancakes!" said Stink.

"Don't tell me. Abe Lincoln ate silver-dollar pancakes," said Judy.

Stink shrugged. "No. But he did eat corn cakes with honey. And sausages. *Not* the talking kind."

"Breakfast for dinner," said Grandma Lou. "I like it. But I have a better idea."

"What could be better than having silver-dollar pancakes?" Stink asked.

"Ghosts in the Hole," said Grandma Lou.

"Ghosts in the Hole?" Stink asked in a whisper.

"You take a piece of bread and cut out the middle with a cookie cutter."

"We used to call them Toads in the Hole!" said Dad.

"We did. And I just happen to have" — Grandma Lou rummaged in her bag — "a ghost-shaped cookie cutter. See? You cook an egg in the middle. We can do it in a skillet over the fire."

"Ghost toast!" said Judy. "I like it!"

"Ghost Toasties!" said Stink.

In no time, Grandma Lou had whipped up ghost toast for everybody. Pugsy ate the one she dropped on the floor.

"My Ghost Toastie is star-ing at me with a creepy yel-low eye," said Stink. "I call it the Eye of the Storm." He stabbed a fork into the Eye of the Storm. Yellow stuff oozed all over his plate. "Dinner, I mean breakfast, is better cooked over a fire. Pass the beans, please." He picked up a spoon, dug in, and ate beans right out of the can.

"Stink, you never liked beans before," said Mom.

"They taste better in a can," said Stink. "Just like how Abe Lincoln ate them."

"Stink, Abe Lincoln didn't even have food in a can. Did he?" Judy asked.

"Yah-huh," said Stink. "They ate stuff from cans in the Civil War. Some guy even invented the can opener back then."

"Yes, but did Abe Lincoln eat *breakfast* for *dinner*?" said Judy.

"No matter how great he was," said Stink, "I'll bet even Abe Lincoln never ate Ghost Toasties while he waited out a hurricane."

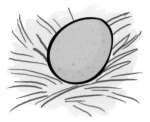

Dinner was over. The Moodys huddled around the fireplace. Orange and blue flames licked the logs, sending spooky shadows dancing across the family room. Outside, the rain made a steady drumbeat on the roof.

"Is it time yet?" asked Stink.

"Is it time yet?" asked Judy.

"It's time," said Mom.

"Time for what?" asked Grandma Lou.

"Time for s'mores!" yelled Judy and Stink. Dad got the long forks. Mom got the chocolate and graham crackers. Stink

and Judy ripped open the marshmallows.

While they roasted marshmallows on sticks over the fire, Grandma Lou said, "S'mores go better with stories. Let's each tell a story."

"You first, Grandma Lou," said Stink. "And make it scary. But not too scary."

"Hmm, let's see," said Grandma Lou. "Oh, I know. Well, this story isn't scary, but it *is* about a hurricane."

"Hurricane story. Cool beans," said Judy.

"When I was a young girl, a little older than Judy, I lived on a farm and—"

"Is this an olden days story?" asked Stink. "Like in Abe Lincoln times?"

"Or an LBS like Dad tells," said Judy. "A Long Boring Story."

"Thanks a lot," said Dad.

"Did you have electricity back then?" Stink asked Grandma Lou. "Because Abe Lincoln didn't."

"Yes, we had electricity," said Grandma Lou. "I'm not quite as old as Abe Lincoln, you know. Anyway, my dad—your great-grandpa—let me raise chickens for my 4-H project. I belonged to the Cluck Club."

"Bwaaaack!" Stink clucked. "Bwack, bwack."

"I had six chickens. One of them— Suzie Q—was very special. When she was just a three-day-old chick, I rescued her from the jaws of our barn cat, Daisy."

"Oopsy-Daisy!" said Judy, and everybody cracked up.

"Suzie Q had blue legs and black tail feathers. I had to hand-feed her because she had a crooked beak. That chicken rode around with me on my bike. She'd hop on my shoulder when I was brushing our horse, Sweet Potato, or read with me.

"I'll never forget the first time she laid an egg. She stood up straight as a statue, raised her head high and—oopsy-daisy—looked as surprised as anyone when out popped a monster egg. Not just any old white egg, either. A blue egg!"

"Whoa. Like an Easter egg?" Stink asked.

"Yes, sirree. That bird laid the most beautiful sky-blue egg you ever set eyes on. I knew right then and there Suzie Q would win me a prize at the county fair.

"Then it happened. One warm, fall day—October 1954, I think it was—wind started whipping around the farm like crazy, blowing over anything that wasn't nailed down. We heard on the radio that Hurricane Annabelle was headed our way.

"Boy, that was some storm. Rained like a river. One-hundred-twenty-mile-an-hour winds. Took the roof right off our toolshed"—Grandma Lou snapped her fingers—"just like that."

At almost the exact same time that Grandma Lou snapped her fingers, the shutters slapped against the house. Stink jumped.

"Hurricanes are serious business," said Grandma Lou. "Folks up in Hampton had reported gusts of a hundred thirty miles an hour. So you can imagine, when Hurricane Annabelle blew in, I was worried about my chickens. Chickens don't even like to get wet."

"Makes them madder than a wet hen," said Dad, laughing at his own joke.

"All the chickens scurried into the coop, except for one."

"Uh-oh," said Judy.

Grandma Lou nodded. "It was my Suzie Q. I looked everywhere for her. By that time I was wet as a drowned rat. My dad made me go back inside the house."

"So what'd you do?" Judy asked.

"I pressed my nose to the window, my eyes glued on that chicken coop, hoping she'd come back. I was plenty angry with my dad for leaving Suzie out there and not letting me go back outside. I'm sure I hardly said three words to him for a whole week!"

"What happened? What happened?" Stink asked. "Did you ever find her?"

"I went to bed. Hardly slept a wink.

Woke up the next morning and every-thing was blown to smithereens. Tree limbs had been tossed around like pick-up sticks. The toolshed was just a pile of toothpicks."

Mom held her breath.

"The chicken coop was gone!"

"What do you mean gone?" Judy asked.

"G-O-N-E gone. Blown from here to Hullabaloo or Timbuktu by Annabelle."

"And Suzie Q?"

"For days after Hurricane Annabelle blew out, I rode around in the back of my dad's truck, searching high and low for that chicken, calling for her, asking everybody we came across if they'd seen a blue-legged, black-tailed chicken with a crooked beak."

"Did you ever find her?" Judy asked.

"Just when I thought I'd never see Suzie Q again, one day, out of the blue, I picked up the newspaper. Right there on the front page was a story about a girl a few towns

over who won first prize at the county fair for a blue egg! The paper said she'd found her prize egg-layer in the hurricane, so they called their blue-legged, black-tailed chicken Annabelle.

"I knew Annabelle had to be my Suzie Q. I could tell by her crooked beak. Not to mention she got herself a first-prize blue ribbon for laying the most beautiful blue egg."

"Did you get her back?" Judy asked.

Grandma Lou's face glowed copper in the firelight. She smiled. "My daddy drove me out there and we met that girl and her family and I'll be gobsmacked if that chicken didn't flap right up onto my shoulder as soon as she saw me.

"I got my Suzie Q back. To this day, I still can't figure out how she ended up a whole three towns over. But that was the power of Hurricane Annabelle."

"The end," said Stink. "That was a long story."

"And it wasn't even boring!" said Judy.

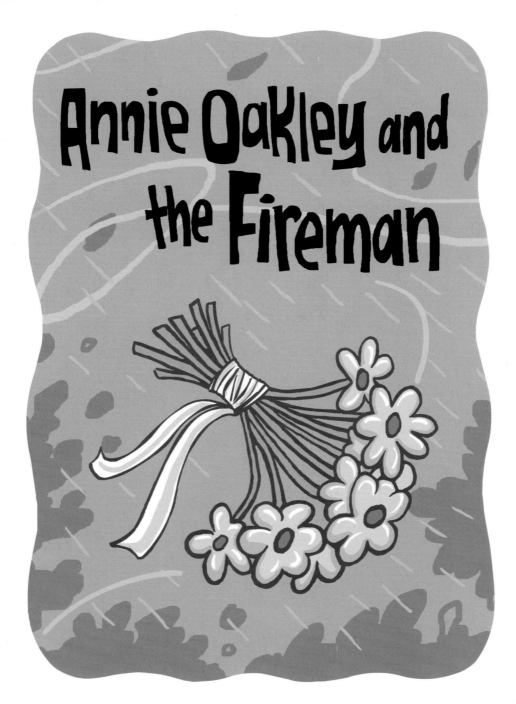

Stink stabbed a marshmallow with his fork. "Let's have *some more* stories with s'mores," he chirped.

Mom smiled at Dad over her glasses. "Dad and I have a story. About our wedding."

"It's the story of how another woman came between us," Dad teased.

Stink's eyes got big. "You mean Mom almost wasn't *Mom*?"

"And *you* almost weren't born," Judy teased.

"Her name was Stacy," said Dad.

"Yech," said Stink.

"*Hurricane* Stacy!" Mom cried.

"Hurricane *Cupid*," said Grandma Lou. She winked.

"Tell us. Tell-us-tell-us-tell-us!" said Stink.

"For the record, an outdoor wedding was your mother's idea," Dad began.

"The day *started out* warm and sunny," said Mom.

"Then all of a sudden," Dad said, "about an hour before the wedding was supposed to begin, the temperature dropped and the wind kicked up. The whole sky went dark."

"Those dark clouds were like a sign,"

said Mom. Stink shuddered as wind howled down the chimney. A prickle went up Judy's back.

"Trees were bending sideways, and all the chairs on the lawn blew over," Dad told them. "By that time, about sixty or seventy guests had already arrived."

"Then the sky opened up," said Mom. "Rain like you've never seen. And I was in my dress! I ran for shelter under the big white tent, where the tables and food were set up for the reception."

"Did Dad see you?" Judy asked. "That's way bad luck!"

"I'll say. I thought the whole wedding was off!" said Mom. "But Dad suggested we have the wedding under the tent, too. Dad and Grandpa Jack rushed to town to get emergency supplies like flashlights and batteries, in case the power went out."

"Bad idea," said Dad, shaking his head.

"The roads were flooding," said Grandma Lou. "There were downed power lines, fallen trees. It was dangerous to be driving around in that."

"So what happened?" asked Stink.

"CRRASHH!" Mom slapped her hands together like a thunderclap. "The rain came down even harder and blew in sideways under the tent. Me and Grandma Lou and my parents and the guests started moving the food from the tent into the old barn. We had saved most of it when — *ker-plunk!* — down came the whole tent."

"Whoa," said Judy.

"By that time, I was drenched," said Mom, "and my dress was ruined. I looked around the barn for something dry to wear. All I could find was a trunk with some old costumes in it."

"Did you dress up like a witch?" Stink asked.

"Or Wonder Woman?" Judy asked.

"Annie Oakley," said Mom. Dad cracked up.

"That's cuckoo-berry!" Stink said.

"That's still not the worst part," said Mom.

"What's the worst part?" asked Judy.

"How can it get any worse?" asked Stink.

"No Dad," said Mom.

Judy twisted a curl of hair. Stink tore at a fingernail.

"Three o'clock. Four o'clock. Five o'clock," said Mom. "Still no Dad."

"Did you get scared to marry Mom and run away?" Stink asked Dad.

"Of course not!" said Dad.

"Did you think Dad had ditched you, Mom?" Judy asked.

"It did cross my mind," said Mom. She twirled her wedding ring back and forth. "But mostly I was scared to death that something had happened to him."

"The power had gone out, too, of course," said Grandma Lou. "No lights, no microphone, no music."

"No wedding," said Mom. "We were all holed up in the barn, just waiting, listening to the storm rage, when—*Blammo!*—off blew the barn doors! I remember seeing cocktail shrimp bobbing and floating like rubber duckies in a puddle."

Dad tossed another log on the fire. Sparks danced up the chimney.

Stink was practically jumping out of his skin. "Dad! Where were you?"

Dad just smiled. "Let Mom tell it."

Mom went on. "I was sure the whole barn was going to blow down like a house of cards. I mean everything else had gone kaplooey, right? That's when, above the howling wind, I heard a siren. It grew closer. And closer. Finally, a fire engine came screaming up the drive. My heart jumped into my throat. I was sure they were coming to tell us that something bad had happened to Dad and Grandpa Jack."

The room got quiet, except for the spitting fire.

"From a loudspeaker on the fire truck came a voice like Darth Vader. The voice said, 'Kate Edison. Will you marry me?'"

Mom's eyes teared up. "I raced out into the pouring rain in my Annie Oakley costume. There was your father, leaning off the fire engine, wearing a giant yellow slicker, a *Little Mermaid* life preserver, and a funny grin."

"You had to mention the life preserver, didn't you?" Dad said, chuckling.

"I burst out crying. I was never so happy to see your dad."

"Grandpa and I had driven the car through some deep water in the road and the engine conked out," Dad explained. "We pushed the car to higher ground and tried forever to get it started. Luckily some firefighters stopped to help. When I said it was my wedding day, well, the rest is history."

Grandma Lou clapped her hands. "Now you kids know the story of how Annie Oakley married a fireman." Stink and Judy laughed.

"So you got married and had us and lived happily ever after?" said Stink.

"And . . . we had cake," said Dad.

"Lots and lots of cake," said Mom. "It was about the only thing that didn't get ruined that day. And the fire truck played its radio over the loudspeaker so Dad and I could have our first dance together."

"The Temptations. 'I Wish It Would Rain.'" Mom and Dad started singing.

"That's a terrible, horrible, no good, very bad story," said Judy. "But the ending makes it so great!"

"Epic!" said Stink. "Hey, wait. Did you say Edison? That's *my* middle name."

"I thought it was Earwig," said Judy.

"Hardee-har-har." Stink made a face

at Judy. "Too bad the *real* Thomas Edison didn't come to your wedding. He could have invented the lightbulb all over again and saved the whole entire wedding!"

Judy snorted.

"From a whirlwind romance to a hurricane wedding," said Grandma Lou.

Stink held out a couch pillow. "Kate, Kate, will you marry me? *Mww, mww, mww.*" He made smooching sounds.

Judy hung a pillowcase from her head for a veil and pretended she was in a wedding march. "Da, da, dah-dah," she sang.

"We still have a piece of that wedding cake," said Mom. "In the freezer."

"*That's* the iceberg in the back of the freezer?" Judy asked.

"What are we waiting for?" Stink asked. "Let's eat it."

"We're saving it for a special occasion," said Dad.

"But this is an emergency," said Stink. "What could be more special than that?"

My turn," said Judy. "I know a hurricane story. It's called Mr. Drybones. But it's a little scary." She peered at Stink.

"Why are you looking at me?" Stink asked. "I'm not scared." He scooched closer to Grandma Lou. She put an arm around him.

"Once there was a hurricane named Elmer that came to Frog Neck Lake, Virginia. The winds blew—*woooooh*—and all the lights went out."

"Just like us!" said Stink.

"Down a dark, dark street called Croaker Road, there was a dark, dark house."

Stink leaned in closer. "That's our house!"

"And the dark, dark house had a dark, dark door. Behind the dark, dark door was a dark, dark hall. And down the dark, dark hall were some dark, dark stairs."

Stink shivered. He twisted the end of a blanket into a tornado of a knot.

"At the top of the dark, dark stairs was an even darker hall. At the end of that dark, dark hall was an even darker door."

Before Judy could say the next line of her story, a door slammed. For real!

Everybody jumped. "It's just the wind," said Dad. Mouse hid under the couch.

"Behind the dark, dark door," Judy went on, "were dark, dark steps that went up to a dark, dark attic. In the dark, dark attic was a dark, dark closet. And in the dark, dark closet was a dark, dark box."

"What's in the box?" Stink asked, his eyes wide.

"From the dark, dark box came a dark, dark rattling sound, like the sound of dry bones. And when the dark, dark box was opened, out came . . ."

Stink covered his eyes with his hands. "Mr. Drybones?" he squeaked.

"No—a pink jellybean!" Judy squealed. Everybody laughed.

"That's a good one," said Dad. "You had *me* a little scared for a minute."

"I wasn't scared. I wasn't scared!" said Stink.

"Sure, Stink," said Judy.

Dad put one last log on the fire. Grandma Lou pulled a blanket up around Stink's shoulders.

"My turn!" said Stink.

"Let's hear your story, Stink," said Mom. "Then bedtime. It's almost ten. Abe Lincoln was in bed every night by nine o'clock," she added slyly.

"For real?" Stink asked.

"It has to be a hurricane story," Judy told him.

"Um, okay, it's a hurricane story," said Stink. "But it's also an Abe Lincoln story."

"Oh, brother," said Judy. "Did they even have hurricanes back then?"

"Yeah. Even Christopher Columbus had one," said Stink.

"It's true," said Dad. "On one of his voyages to the New World."

"And don't forget Ben Franklin," said Mom. "He went out to study an eclipse one night and ended up studying a hurricane."

"Sorry I asked!" said Judy. "I thought it was a day *off* from school, that's all."

"So. Is everybody ready or not?" asked Stink.

"Ready, Freddy," said Judy.

"Once upon a time, Abe Lincoln sat in his log cabin, reading a book."

"Don't tell me. By candlelight," said Judy.

"By candlelight. There was a monster storm outside. We're talking super bad, like it could have been Hurricane Hercules. Abe rocked back and forth, back and forth in his rocking chair, reading, when . . . *Brrinngg!*"

Judy jumped.

"The phone rang," said Stink.

"Wait," said Judy. "Abe Lincoln had *a phone*?"

Grandma Lou put her finger to her lips. "Let's let Stink have his turn."

Stink pretended to pick up a phone. "'Hello?' Abe said. A spooky voice on the other end said, 'The Viper is coming, the Viper is coming. The Viper is just down the road.'

"'Who is the Viper? And why are you coming?' Abe asked.

"*Click.* The phone went dead.

"Abe went back to reading. But he hadn't even read two sentences when—*Brrinngg!*—the telephone rang again. 'Helllooo?' Abe said, all shaky-like.

"'The Viper is coming. The Viper is

coming for you. The Viper is on your street.'

"Presidents are always super brave, but even tall Abe was a little scared now. 'Who is the Viper? And why are you coming for me?'

"*Click.* The phone went dead. Again.

"Abe was super-scared now. He rocked back and forth, back and forth in his rocking chair when—*Brrinngg!*—the phone rang. *Again.*"

"Not again," said Judy.

"'Not again!' said Abe. He picked up the phone. 'Helllooo?'

"'The Viper is coming. The Viper is coming. The Viper is almost at your door.'

"Now Abe was shaking in his slippers, he was so scared. But before he could ask, 'Who is the Viper?' one more time, he heard a loud *Boom! Boom! Boom!*

"It wasn't a Toad Pee tent that landed on his roof. It wasn't a spaceship or a bionic squirrel either. It was a knock. On his door!" Stink paused. He looked right at Judy. In a spooky voice, he asked, "Should Abe answer the door?"

"Yes!" yelled Judy. "No, wait. No!"

"No. Of course not. But if Abe wanted to be president someday, he had to be brave. So he got up and opened the door a crack. *CREEEAK!*

"Abe peeked out the door. There on his

doorstep was a short, funny-looking man with a bucket in one hand and a sponge in the other."

"Sponge Bob?" Judy whispered.

Stink's eyes grew wide. He shook his head no. He threw out his hands and shouted, "'I am the Viper!'"

Everybody jumped. Mouse leaped from under the couch into Judy's arms. Judy let out a squeal.

"'Who are you?' said Abe. 'And what do you want with me?'

"'I told you. I am the Viper. The Vindow Viper. I come to vipe your vindows!'"

91

The next morning, when Judy came downstairs, Stink was sprawled on the floor writing in a notebook with his five-in-one flashlight pen.

"What are you doing?" Judy asked.

"Writing a novel," said Stink. "With my hurricane pen—it has a built-in flashlight. The power's still out. My book's going to be thirty-nine pages long. Want to hear?"

"Sure!" said Judy. She sat down. She

closed her eyes and got ready to listen with her best third-grade listening ears that she usually saved for school days.

Stink began. "'It was a dark and stormy night.'"

Silence. More silence. Judy opened one eye. She opened the other eye.

"Go on," said Judy. "I'm listening."

"That's all I have so far," said Stink.

"Only thirty-eight and three-quarters more pages to go," said Judy.

"Thirty-eight and a half," said Stink, "if I write really big."

"Where's Grandma Lou?"

"Everybody's out in the car," said Stink. "Listening to the radio."

Mom and Dad came back in. "No school again today," said Mom.

"Yes!" Stink pumped his arm in the air.

"Good news," said Dad. "They downgraded the storm from Category Three to Category Two."

@ @ @

Hurricane Elmer. Day two. Grandma Lou taught Judy how to knit with just her fingers. She showed Stink how to mummy-wrap his own hands. They had stare-down contests. They had thumb-wrestling contests. Then Grandma Lou pulled out her fortune-telling game.

"You brought your Ouija board!" said Judy.

"What's a weejie board?" asked Stink.

"It's not for scaredy-cats," said Judy. "It's for talking to ghosts. And for telling fortunes."

"And it glows in the dark," said Grandma Lou. "You kids go ahead and play while I finish my knitting."

"So how does it work?" asked Stink, leaning in to see.

"We rest our fingers on the pointer— lightly—and ask it a question. Then it spells out the answer. Or it says *Yes, No,* or *Good bye.*"

Judy and Stink placed their finger-tips on the pointer. "Me first," said Stink. "What is Judy's middle name?" The pointer spelled out letters one by one.

R-A-T-F-A-C-E.

"*Rat face!* No fair, Stink. You made it say that," said Judy.

"Did not!"

"Okay," said Judy. "My turn. What is Stink's middle name?"

"P . . ."

"Wrong! My middle name starts with an E."

The pointer moved to the letter *U.* "P-U," said Judy.

"P-U what?" said Stink.

"That's it. P.U. is your middle name, Stinker."

"Is not," said Stink. "You made it spell that."

Judy shrugged. "I have a question for real. Will we have school tomorrow?"

The pointer zoomed up to the right-hand corner of the board, where the word *NO* was printed. "NO," said Judy.

"YAY!" said Stink.

"Stink, quit moving it."

"I'm not—"

"Guess what, kids," said Mom, coming into the room. "No school tomorrow either. I just got a robo-call on my cell phone from the superintendent's office."

Judy and Stink locked eyes. Judy got goose bumps. Stink shivered.

"We already know," said Stink. "A ghost just told us."

"The Ghost of Weejie," said Judy.

"Any chance your ghost could tell us when the power's coming back on?" Mom asked, raising an eyebrow.

"Okay," said Judy. "But, Stink, you can't move it this time."

"I won't! Cross my heart and spit in my eye!"

"Grandma Lou," said Judy, "will you watch to make sure Stink doesn't move the pointer?"

"Okay," said Grandma Lou. "But make it quick. It's almost time for my nap."

"Weejie," said Stink, "is there a ghost in Judy's room?"

Just then, Mouse pounced on the board and the pointer slid down to *GOOD BYE*.

100

"That doesn't count," said Stink. "Mouse moved it."

"Okay. Try again."

"Is there a ghost in Judy's room?" Stink asked.

The pointer moved toward the number two. Then the pointer went to the letter M. After that it made a beeline for the word *YES*.

"I didn't move it," said Stink. "Honest."

"Me either." Judy's eyes grew wide. "Grandma Lou, I wouldn't take a nap if I were you. Weejie says there's a ghost in my room. And you're sleeping in there."

"I'm not afraid of a silly old ghost," said Grandma Lou.

"You're not?" Judy asked.

"Nope. I grew up in an old house with a ghost."

"You did?" Stink asked.

"Sure. His name was Bob. He liked pretzels."

"Bob? Ghosts don't have the name Bob," said Judy.

"Why not? What name do you think they have? Casper?"

"I don't know. Ichabod. Or Bloody Mary or something."

"Or Abe Lincoln," said Stink. "Some people think his ghost is in the White House. But ghosts aren't real. And they definitely don't eat pretzels."

"How do you know, if you've never seen one?" said Grandma Lou with a twinkle in her eye. "If Santa likes cookies, why can't Bob like pretzels?"

Stink scratched his head. Stink scratched his elbow. Suddenly, Stink felt itchy and scratchy all over.

"Yep, old One-Legged Bob. We'd hear him clomping around the attic at night, dancing on one leg. Could hardly sleep a wink some nights."

"You're just saying that," Stink said to Grandma Lou.

"Am I?"

"Did Bob ever go bowling up there?" Judy asked.

Stink shook off a shiver. "Dad!" he called to the next room. "Grandma Lou's teasing us with scares. About ghosts."

Dad poked his head into the room. "Grandma Lou sure is a good storyteller, isn't she, kids?"

"Now I'm going to warm up some milk over the fire and go upstairs to take my nap," said Grandma Lou.

Naps. Ghosts. Pretzels. She, Judy Moody, had an idea.

Rare!

Judy hurry-up whispered her idea to Stink. They raced upstairs.

"Stink, go get a pair of Dad's shoes. And your hurricane pen. And some pretzels. Hurry, before Grandma Lou comes up to take her nap."

Stink didn't even mind Judy bossing him. Pranking Grandma Lou was going to be even better than the Fake Hand in the Toilet joke.

Judy got the periscope from her room—the one she had made from coffee cans, oatmeal containers, and tissue boxes—and leaned it up against the wall in the hall so it would be ready. Next, she tied a piece of thread to a single pretzel and put it with other pretzels on a plate on the nightstand. She flicked the five-in-one pen to make sure it worked.

She, Judy Moody, with Stink's help, was going to ghost Grandma Lou good.

"Hey, how about sound effects?" Stink said, coming back with Dad's boots. "I have a bunch on the computer."

"Stink. Blackout. Remember? We'll have to make our own sound effects. Go get one of Mom's fancy water glasses—but don't let her see you take it."

Judy and Stink rigged up the greatest

ghost trick ever. Then they hid in Stink's room and waited. Stink could hear Judy breathing. It sounded a little like a ghost. A chill crept across his back.

"I think I hear her," said Stink.

"Shh! Here she comes."

Grandma Lou went into Judy's room and closed the door. Judy and Stink counted to a hundred. Twice.

"Ghost time!" Judy whispered. She motioned Stink to follow her into the hallway.

Stink made one-legged clomping sounds outside Judy's room with a boot of Dad's. Judy scratchy-scratch-scratched on the wall and tappa-tap-tapped on the bedroom door.

No answer. Grandma Lou must have fallen asleep.

"I don't think she heard our ghost," Judy whispered.

Stink mimed opening the door a little. Judy turned the knob and slowly opened the door a crack. Stink made creaky-door sounds with his best squeaky-door voice, as if a ghost were entering the room.

Judy pushed her periscope through the crack. She spied on Grandma Lou.

"Milo, Candy Cane, did you hear something?" they heard Grandma Lou ask. "No? I guess it was just my imagination."

"Cue the ghost," whispered Judy.

Stink wet his finger with spit and rubbed it around the rim of the fancy water glass. *Weeeee! Wooooo!* The glass made ghosty, goose-bumpy sounds. Even Judy got the shivers.

"Did you hear *that*?" they heard Grandma Lou ask the animals. "No? Okay. I guess I'll go back to sleep."

"Cue the pretzel," Judy whispered. Stink oh-so-carefully pulled on the end of the string. *CRASH!* The whole plate of pretzels fell to the floor, except for one. One pretzel walked across the floor and out the door.

"A walking pretzel? Now that's strange," they heard Grandma Lou say. "Unless it's a . . . No. Couldn't be."

And now, for the icing on the cake, thought Judy. Stink handed her his flashlight pen. Judy turned on the pointer. A small green beam of light shot out like a laser. Through the open crack in the door, Judy slowly spelled out three letters on the wall of her room for Grandma Lou to see.

B-O-B.

"Ghost!" they heard Grandma Lou screech. "Ghost in the house! Bob is back!"

Through the periscope, Judy saw Grandma Lou jump up in bed.

"Quick! Hide the stuff!" she whisper-yelled to Stink. Stink tossed the ghost supplies into his room. Judy tried to hide the periscope behind her back.

Grandma Lou grabbed Milo and

Candy Cane and dashed out into the hall, almost crashing into Judy and Stink.

"Grandma Lou," said Judy, "you look like you just saw a ghost!"

"G-g-ghost!" Grandma Lou pointed toward Judy's room. "It's Bob. He's baaaaack!"

"Ghost? There's no such thing as ghosts," said Stink.

"Pretzels don't just up and walk by themselves," hissed Grandma Lou. "I told you, ghosts *love* pretzels."

Judy snickered. Stink bit his cheeks to keep from laughing.

Grandma Lou narrowed her eyes. "Wait just a cotton-candy-eatin' second. I see a ghost and—why aren't you two scared? You're up to something, aren't you?"

Judy shook her head. Stink tried to keep a straight face. But he couldn't hold it in for one more second.

"It was us!" Stink cried.

CHOMP! Judy bit into a pretzel and grinned.

"The pretzel-eating ghost is Judy. And me!" Stink cried. "We pranked you! We ghost-pranked you so good!" Judy and Stink rolled on the ground, laughing.

Hummm. *Click. Purrrr.* Stink woke with a start. Something was different. Something was not right. "Judy!" he said rubbing his eyes. "Did you hear sounds?"

"Umm. Ghost," said a sleepy Judy.

"It's not a ghost. I hear humming. And clicking."

"House sounds, Stink. Go back to sleep."

Stink reached over and flipped a switch. The light blinked on-off-on-off.

"Hey!" Judy said, squinting.

"Power's back on," said Stink. "No more blackout!"

They padded into the hall. Mom and Dad were up, too. "We left some lights and things on when the power went out," said Mom.

"I'll check the downstairs," said Dad. "You kids go back to bed."

"But I'm not sleepy now," said Stink. "It's too exciting!"

"It's the middle of the night, Stink," said Judy, yawning.

"Warm milk?" Mom asked.

Everybody piled downstairs. Mom heated milk—not on the fire. Judy read her book—not by candlelight. Stink flipped the light switch. On, off. On, off. On. Because he could.

"Yes, Stink. Electricity is a wonderful thing," said Mom. "But don't waste it."

"Think of all the stuff we did this week without electricity," said Judy.

"Are you kidding?" said Stink. "Lights and stuff are like the greatest invention ever. Thank you, Thomas Edison." Blink-blink. Blink-blink-blink.

⊚   ⊚   ⊚

Grandma Lou slept through all the excitement. When she came downstairs in the morning, it had stopped raining and the sky was clearing. "Know what I love most about the storm being over?" she said.

"The *Mad Muskrats* physics-based castle demolition game?" said Stink.

"A warm bubble bath?" said Mom.

"No more beans in a can?" said Dad.

"It's *after* the storm clears." Grandma Lou nodded at the window. A watery sun shone through the clouds. "Just look up at the sky. I bet you'll see a—"

"Rainbow!" Stink called.

"Double rainbow!" Judy called.

Judy, Stink, and Grandma Lou rushed outside. They blinked in the cloudy-bright light. Tree branches and snapped twigs littered the lawn. The roof of the shed had peeled back like a cereal-box top. The mailbox had turned into a twisty straw.

Judy tilted her head to the sky. "A double rainbow is way lucky. Luckier than a lucky penny."

"Make a wish," said Grandma Lou.

"I wish we could go out in the kayak," said Judy.

"Yeah, I wish we could go for a ride in *Gert* before Dad makes us clean up the yard," said Stink.

"Follow me," said Grandma Lou.

Before you could say *It was a dark and stormy night,* Grandma Lou, Judy, and Stink had slipped into life vests and were paddling around a "lake" in the back-yard. Ducks floated in puddles and frogs kicked up a chorus.

"I can't believe we're in a boat—on a

lake in the middle of the backyard!" said Stink. "Pretend we're surfing the rapids on a river in the Grand Canyon."

"How's it feel?" asked Grandma Lou.

"Like I'm a tub toy."

"It's like we're floating on a river of chocolate milk," said Judy.

"The creek swelled up so high, it flooded the backyard," said Grandma Lou.

Stink pointed to a shoe floating past. "Hey! Isn't that my sneaker?"

"And there's my soccer ball," said Judy. "The pink-and-black one that's been up on the roof since last summer!"

"We're lucky," said Grandma Lou. "People lose cars, houses, pets in these storms. One year the wind was so bad, my neighbor's playhouse ended up in a tree."

"A tree house!" said Stink.

"I know the storm's over—and we should be happy that it wasn't a lot worse—but I feel sadder than ABC gum on the bottom of the pool," Judy said.

"I feel bluer than a mutant frog," said Stink.

"Sorry to hear that," said Grandma Lou. "Want to talk about it?"

"It's over," said Stink. "No more storm."

"No more blackout," said Judy.

"It was fun without electricity. But now there will never be another Hurricane Elmer," said Stink.

"Back to school," said Judy.

"And homework," said Stink.

"And now you and Pugsy'll be going home, too, Grandma Lou," said Judy.

"Everybody will go back to watching TV and playing games on the computer like we did before," said Stink. "No more stories. No more s'mores."

"Tell you what," said Grandma Lou. "You can come visit me anytime, and we'll have a Great Big Blackout of our own. We'll turn out all the lights and cook over a fire and tell stories and eat beans straight out of the can."

"It'll be just like Earth Hour!" said Judy.

"What's Earth Hour?" Stink asked.

"It's when millions of hundreds of

126

people all over the world turn out the lights on purpose at the same time for one hour," said Judy.

"To show that we can work together to save energy," said Grandma Lou.

"They even turn out the lights on Big Ben and the Empire State Building and the Eiffel Tower and—"

"Okay, Judy. I get it!" said Stink.

"Dare to save the planet, Stink," said Judy.

"I will if you will," said Stink. He turned to Grandma Lou. "But we don't have to wait for Earth Hour, do we?"

"We can have our own Earth Hour, too," said Grandma Lou.

"Or Earth *Two* Hours," said Judy.

"With stories and s'mores?" Stink asked.

"And Musical Board Games and everything?" said Judy.

"But no ghosts," said Stink.

"No ghosts," agreed Grandma Lou.

"Not even Ghost Toasties?" Judy asked.

"Well, maybe Ghost Toasties," said Grandma Lou.

"Do you swear?" asked Stink. "On *Gert*?"

Judy and Stink put their heads together and whispered.

"Grandma Lou," said Judy, "Stink and I would like you to take the Ghost-Toastie Oath."

"The Ghost-Toastie Oath, huh?"

"Raise your right hand," said Judy.

Grandma Lou put down her paddle and raised her right hand.

"Repeat after us," said Stink.

"I, Grandma Louise Moody," said Judy.

"I, Grandma Louise Moody," said Grandma Lou.

"Do solemnly swear," said Judy.

"Do solemnly swear," said Grandma Lou.

"That we will have a fake great big blackout . . ."

"That we will have a fake great big blackout . . ."

"The next time Judy and Stink visit."

"The next time Judy and Stink visit."

"And it will be just as fun as Elmer."

"And it will be just as fun as Elmer," said Grandma Lou.

"When we get back to the house, we'll write it down on paper and you can sign it in blood," said Stink.

"Will ketchup do?" asked Grandma Lou.

"Stink, she can just spit to make it official."

"Tell you what," said Grandma Lou. "How about a pinky handshake?"

"A three-way pinky promise?" asked Judy.

"A triple-pinky swear!" said Stink.

"It'll be our very own secret hand-shake," said Grandma Lou.

Each of them stuck out a little finger.

The three locked pinkies. "Triple dare pinky swear!" they said all together.

Grandma Lou's eyes danced. "That should seal the deal." She gave them one last sideways squeeze before turning the kayak around. "Pugsy and I look forward to it."

"So, Grandma Lou," said Stink, "got any plans for next weekend?"

SCREAM LIKE A MONKEY

WILD CARD ?

JUMP 4 ...SPACES

ROLL AGAIN

SKIP 3 SPACES

PICK A CARD

EXTRA TURN

LOSE A TURN

Stuff to Do in a Big Bad Blackout:

1. Read a book by candlelight, flashlight, or headlamp.

2. Break out a board game or a deck of cards.

3. Tell not-so-scary scary stories. And knock-knock jokes.

4. Get a piece of string or yarn. Tie it into a loop and play cat's cradle.

5. Shine a flashlight onto a wall and make shadow puppets with your hands. *Quack, boo, hippety-hop!*

WIN!

START

PICK A CARD

LOS...

6. *I'm thinking of a game to play in the dark.*
Twenty questions . . .

7. Play the Quiet Game. See who can last the
longest without a peep, squeak, or giggle.

8. Get your Picasso on. Draw a picture in the
dark (no peeking!) and see if family and
friends can guess what your masterpiece is.

9. Name the yellow bone fame. Oops—that's
play the telephone game!